SCIENCE FICTION
INHABITANTS OF MARS
AN INTERESTING STORY OF 2080AD
DURGA PRAMANIK

PRODUCT

Description : - Will we not be able to go to earth again? My mind is getting very nervous. Don't know how people will be able to survive there! One, many cities and countries have already been destroyed in that fierce nuclear war. Millions of people have been killed along with countless organisms and then due to the rising temperature of the planet, if any creature or human survives then it will be a big deal. But even if he survives, what will he eat? There, now even grass cannot grow in some places because nuclear radiation has spread there. That green earth is now going to be completely deserted. People will also have to face a food crisis.

 So ! what to us; We are safe now because we are on Mars and we have made it our new abode. Right now we are living in tunnels and I believe. In the days to come, I and my people together will make it better than the earth. Professor Belen was discussing this topic with his people sitting inside the tunnels. They were all within a very large tunnel where they had created many such large and small tunnels on Mars.

Where all the things needed for living were made. Such an artificial environment where life can be lived like the earth, a house to live in and a field for farming. It was as if food items were also being grown by agriculture.

Like being in a very big ship in an ocean. Who keeps circling the ocean for months and a city is settled within it! In which thousands of people are living happily. They had made all the facilities there for themselves which were necessary for human beings and all were working day and night unitedly towards a long mission. They believed that they would make the entire planet Earth-like one day and create a new human civilization called the people of Mars.

This story is just a fictional story of the successful efforts and hard work of scientists in starting life on Mars, which is very exciting and informative. Through this story, you will be able to understand the time cycle of history and give wings to your imagination on the possibilities of life on Mars. In this story, a boy suddenly comes to Mars, which is millions of light years away from the Solar System, a planet which is exactly like our Earth. That earth also completes the period like our earth is doing. The people there are very intelligent and technical, which is many times more than us. When that boy gets a signal on his spaceship about the presence of some people on Mars, he reaches there to meet them and gives a lot of information about his planet to the people of Earth. On Mars, with his artistic skills, very soon the environment becomes adapted for life. He gets a new civilization built on Mars. It also helps in improving the deteriorating environment on the earth. In this way, he starts a new space age, so that by reducing the time and distance, it can be reached from one planet to another very soon. Hope this futuristic fictional story of the search for life on Mars will amuse you a lot. Thank you!

Table of contents

Introduction:- This story is just a fictional story of the successful efforts and hard work of scientists in starting life on Mars, which is very exciting and informative too. Through this story, you will be able to understand the time cycle of history and give wings to your imagination on the possibilities of life on Mars. In this story, a boy suddenly comes to Mars, which is millions of light years away from the solar system, from an Earth which is exactly like our Earth. That earth also completes the period like our earth is doing. The people there are very intelligent and technical, which is many times more than us. When that boy gets a signal on his spaceship about the presence of some people on Mars, he reaches there to meet them and gives a lot of information about his planet to the people of Earth. With his art skills on Mars, very soon the atmosphere becomes adapted for life.

He gets a new civilization built on Mars. It also helps in improving the deteriorating environment on earth. In this way, he starts a new space age, so that by reducing the time and distance, it can be reached from one planet to another very soon. Hope this futuristic fictional story of the search for life on Mars will amuse you a lot.

Author:- This story is written by Durga Pramanik who is a fictional storyteller. This is the fifth story written by him. Due to the increasing impact of climate change and global warming, the author tried to write such stories so that awareness could be created in the public about environmental protection. The author himself is also an activist of a small voluntary organization which is interested in working towards this. The author's only aim in writing this story is to bring public awareness to the environment and to serve human beings.

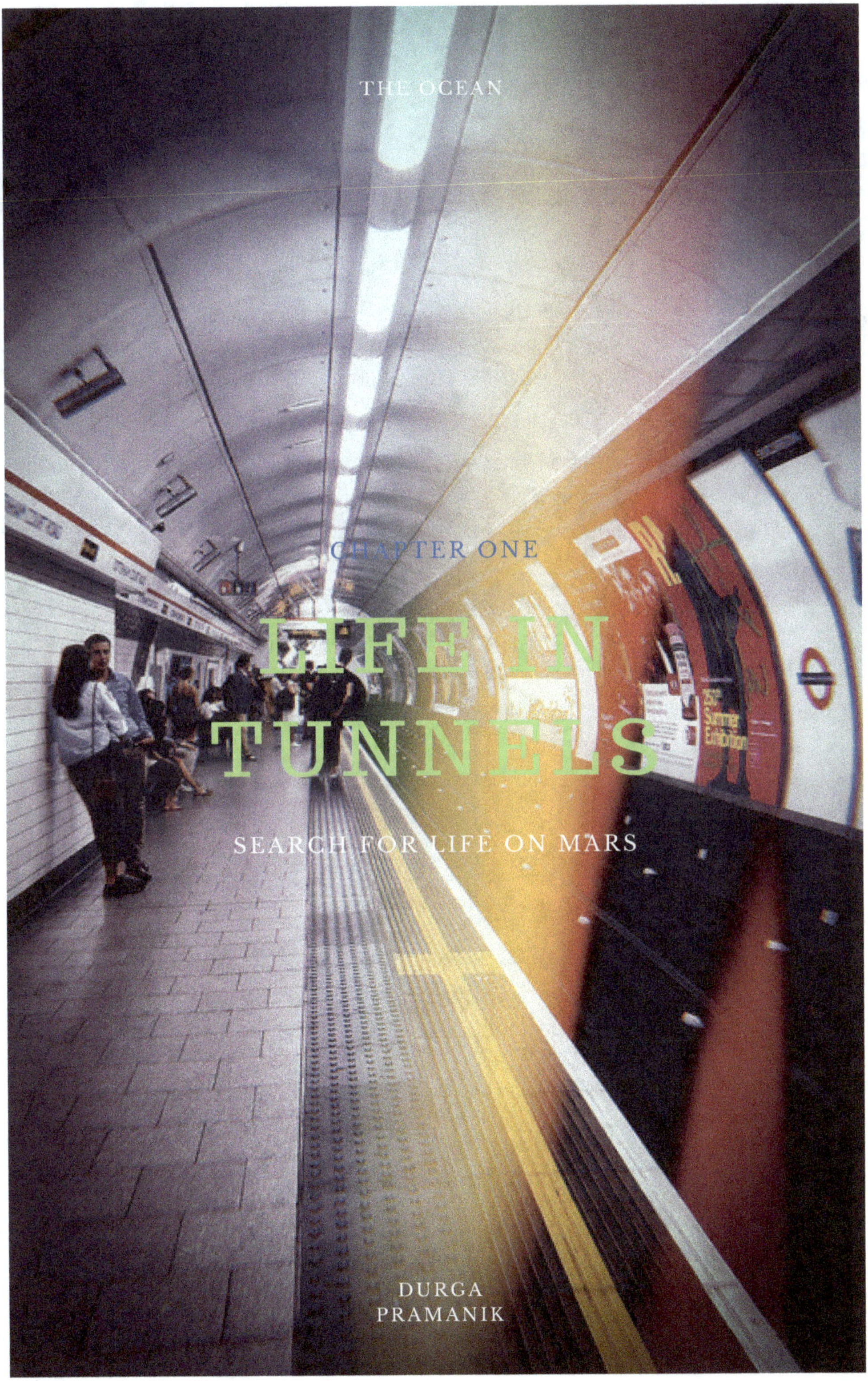

CHAPTER ONE

LIFE IN TUNNELS

SEARCH FOR LIFE ON MARS

DURGA
PRAMANIK

Chapter:- 1

life in the tunnels

Shall we not be able to go to earth again; My mind is getting very nervous. Don't know whether a single person will be able to survive there or not! One is that many cities and countries have already been destroyed in that fierce nuclear war and millions of people have died along with countless creatures. Then due to the increasing temperature of the planet, it would be a big deal if any one organism or human survived. But even if he survives, he will eat, and will not even grow grass there now because that green earth is now going to be completely deserted. So! We are safe now because we are on Mars and we have made it our new abode. At present we are living life in tunnels but in the coming days, my people and I together will make it better than the earth.

LIFE ON
MARS

Professor Belen was discussing with his men. They were all within a very large tunnel where they had created many such large and small tunnels on Mars. Where there was everything to live. Such an artificial environment where life can be lived like the earth, a house to live in and a field for farming. Food was also being grown by farming, as if in a big ship in an ocean! Who keeps circling the ocean for months and a city is settled within it! In which thousands of people are living happily. He had made for himself - 'there all the facilities which were necessary for human beings and were working day and night united towards a long mission to make the whole planet one day like the earth and a new human civilization. Build those who are called the Vashi of Mars. It was early morning, and the rays of the sun had gone out.

Professor Belen and some of his companions were sitting inside a tunnel discussing some things. Like Earth, time moves on Mars. Day and night are almost similar to the earth itself and many more things that show the possibilities of life here. For this reason, scientists have considered it the second planet of the future after Earth. Where human civilization can be saved.

According to the Earth's calendar, it was the month of January and the year was 2080 AD. Understanding the deteriorating condition of the earth, some people worked very hard to keep the human civilization alive on Mars and after a long wait, they got some success. He succeeded in building a spacecraft and even reached Mars. There too, many artificial tunnels were constructed in such a way that when viewed from the inside, it is as if it is like the atmosphere of our earth. They built each of the tunnels like small glass houses. Inside those tunnels, farms along with houses were also made where grains and vegetables could be grown for food. Meaning all those things which are necessary for human beings. The whole life of the people living in those tunnels can also be easily cut, similar facilities were made by those scientists with their hard work.

He had also taken many people from the earth and settled inside those tunnels. They were all such people who were skilled in their field, some were well versed in forest plants, some were related to soil and fossils, some were doctors in substances and some were good with metals. All of them were doctors of some subject or the other. Those who were selected and sent to settle life on Mars.

Professor Belen was the head of all of them, under his supervision all of them were doing research there. Their number was in the thousands. He was given the responsibility of finding life on Mars as soon as possible and establishing life there.

CHAPTER - 2
IMPACT OF CARBON
SPREAD ON EARTH

BUDUCNOS
BL
"Be A PART OF
THE
SOLUTION
NOT PART OF
THE
POLLUTION"

Chapter : - 2

impact of carbon spread on earth

Then one-day Professor Belen's concern for the earth was coming more and more into his mind.

"Sir, do you know how long it will take us when we do a new test here? - John Cate," (Belene's assistant scientist) Now only a few days are left for the weather in the western region to change. The hydrogen bomb we detonated there five years ago is now successful. The soil containing ferrous oxide there has been decomposed into other substances by the reaction. Now the soil of that area will be just like the earth and very soon we will be able to grow trees and plants. We will build a very big forest there, then the atmosphere will be created like the earth and we will all be able to move out of these tunnels and roam in the open air. This planet will become a beautiful planet, there will be greenery all around. We just have to wait for a few more days then our dream will be fulfilled.

"Professor Belen, - Kate, you just made a good point that is easing my anxiety". If the heat on the earth continues to increase rapidly and it cannot be controlled, then we can save selected creatures and humans from there by bringing them here. By the way, many cities have been destroyed so far, many have been submerged and many more are going to happen. If the people of the earth had known about this in time, then such situations would not have happened today. A lot would have been fine, but people's carelessness towards the environment has burnt the earth today with the heat of carbon. It gradually grew so much that it became very difficult to stop it.

The heads of many countries occasionally expressed concern about this and signed the Paris Agreement. Keeping a meeting there every year, I tried to tell my people that I attended that meeting. Even if people were successful in winning the trust of the people, they would have gotten the votes of the people for this. They would make and implement some rules to reduce global warming in their country, which would remain only the coverage of newspapers and TV news channels and nothing else. Some countries had taken some concrete steps, but still what could have happened? You must have heard a proverb - "The gram alone does not break". If all the countries and the citizens of all the countries together would try to reduce carbon from the very beginning. If we had strictly implemented the zero carbon emission rule in our countries and followed it, then such a situation would not have happened today. Millions of lives would have been saved which have been lost only because of their carelessness and are going to go further. Well, this fear also allowed us to search for life on Mars, but the carelessness of the people of the earth was wrong and from above the nuclear war took millions of lives, ruined many countries, and destroyed the soil there. Filled with radiation, it is very difficult to grow even a single grass there.

CHAPTER : - 3
TIME CYCLE

Chapter: - 3
What is a time cycle

Searches on Mars or discoveries on other planets continue to happen anyway and will continue to happen. I agree with this view.

Professor, what will happen with repentance when the bird has eaten the farm proverb - "Jon Kate" - yes you are right but what should we do now? Let us first complete the work which has been assigned to us here.

'Jon Kate, Sir Belen, do you know anything about the cycle of time?' Why? Why this cycle? Suddenly coming to your mind. No, I have heard that time also works on the principle of zero, from where it starts and stops again - 'Jon Kate'. Professor Belen, mean! Meaning! That now life will begin on Mars and long before the end of life on Earth, such things have been written in many books. Especially in the religious books of Hindus, every event has been told in great detail and many things turned out to be true.

The Hindu sages knew all the future events thousands of years in advance. The way we tell the time in four parts, such as the Copper Age, bronze age, Iron Age and golden age, in the same way, he has also described the time cycle in complete detail in a very precise way.

There was one such sage whose name was Ved Vyas who wrote the Bhavishya Purana which tells all the events of today and the events of the whole earth from the first to the next. I am hearing this for the first time, just tell it in detail, come sit and tell - 'Professor Jon'.

So listen Professor, I try to tell you in full detail -

According to Shri Thakur Prasad, who was an astrologer, the period of Hindus has been divided into four parts. Where God has saved this earth by taking birth or manifesting itself in various forms. Earth is the only planet in this solar system where life is possible. Hindu historical periods tell this thing about what happened in which period and how God Himself manifests and saves it when any calamity comes on this earth.

God Means Can you give any exact meaning of this word John Kate As far as I understand it to mean God which we cannot see. Can we think of them as modern-day aliens - 'Professor John asked Kate'?

No, Professor aliens are made by him. In a way, we have also become the inhabitants of this planet in the present, but for the people of other planets, we can only be considered aliens. We can call aliens or living beings of any other planet, whereas God is para-physical.

They are beyond this elemental knowledge, we can consider them to be a very subtle metaphysical element spread throughout the universe, which has neither beginning nor end and is capable and limitless to accept any physical or any other subtle form anytime anywhere. You can understand the masters of powers. Earth is his very favorite planet where he always appears in some form or the other, whatever the reason. It is said that the time of his first appearance was the time of Satyug.

CHAPTER : - 4
KRISTY

Chapter : - 4

Kristy or Satyug

It started on Kartik Shukla Navami Wednesday, Shravan Nakshatra, Dhriti Yoga took place at the time of midday. Its age including the treaty was another 17,28000 human years. Matsya, Kachhap, Varaha, and Narasimha were four inhuman incarnations.

Matsya Avatar- Influence happened in Samvatsar, Chaitra Krishna Panchami, Mool Nakshatra and Siddhi Yoga on Wednesday evening. This incarnation happened to kill the demon Shankhasura and save the Vedas. Kachchpavtar- Jyeshtha Krishna Dashami in Vibhava Samvatsara took place on Sunday in Rohini Nakshatra Dhriti Yoga in the evening. This incarnation took place to lift the weight of the earth and reduce the burden of others and give happiness to others.

Varaha Avatar took place on Chaitra Krishna Trayodashi Sunday, Dhanishta Nakshatra, Brahmayoga in the afternoon of Shukla Samvatsar. This incarnation happened to merge into the ocean of the earth and kill the demon Hiranyaksha for liberation. Narasimha Avatar- In Angira Samvatsar, on Vaishakh Shukla Sunday, in Vishaka Nakshatra in the evening of Variyan Yoga, Hiranyakashipu was killed for the protection of Prahlad.

satyug system
Sin 0 (zero) in Satyuga, Virtue 20 (world) Man's age of one lakh years, body height 21 hands, golden vessel, the behaviour of gems, worldly life in humans, divine food, Pushkar pilgrimage, religion in Satyug all around. He was resting on the ground with his feet. Ikshvaku, Mandhata, Muchukunda, Bhairav Nandaka, Andhaka, Hiranyaksha, Hiranyakashyap, Prahlad, Virochana, Bali, Banasura, Kapil, Kapil Bhadra became kings. His speed was in all three worlds. All of them were worshipers of Brahma. The subjects were ready to obey, eaters of divine food. They used to wear divine clothes.

If he committed a single sin, his country would have been destroyed. Brahmins were scholars of the Vedas. Satyavrat used to participate in Ish Puja. There was power in giving blessings, curses, and grace. Women were respected, and cows gave milk of their own free will. Trees were always plentiful, with rivers brimming with water, fruits and flowers. Solar eclipse 32000, lunar eclipse 5000. All men were true and righteous.

CHAPTER : - 5
GREATEST PERIOD

Beginning of Tretayuga

Tretayuga- Vaishakh Shukla 3 Thursday, started in Rohini Nakshatra and Dhriti Yoga. Vamana, Parashurama and Rama were the three incarnations of that God. The age of Tretayuga including a treaty was 12,96000 human years. In Tretayuga Dharma was established for three stages on the earth.

Vamanavatar was born on Friday to Shravana Nakshatra and Shobhana Yoga Sarvajit Samvatsar. While performing a yajna in this era, Lord Vamana sent King Bali to Hades by donating three steps of the earth. Parashuramavatar- Sarvajit Samvatsar, Vaishakh Shukla Tuesday, Purvabhadrapada Nakshatra, happened in Variyan Yoga. This incarnation took place for the destruction of the proud Kshatriyas and the protection of the devotees.

Ramavatar- Taran Samvatsar, Chaitra Shukla Naumi was born on Thursday in Punarvasu Nakshatra, Sukarma Yoga, in Cancer ascendant in the form of Dasharatha's son in the midday period. This incarnation happened to kill Ravana. Age system - Treta has sin 5, virtue 15 (world) man's age is 10,000 years, body height 14 hands, silver utensils, gold dravya, Ashtagata prana, Naimisharanya pilgrimage, women were virtuous. Rudra solar eclipse 3200, lunar eclipse 500. All the people were virtuous in religion and action. Suryavanshi king in EC.

Treat-
1. Manu,
2. Smoke,
3. Vikukshi,
4. Kati Harishchandra,
5. Rohitashva,
6. Sagar,
7. Munj,
8. equilateral,
9. Veer Bhagirath,
10. Dileep,
11. Raghu,
12. Aja,
13. Dasharatha,
14. Adi Ramachandra,
15. Kush,
16. Agnivarna,
17. Meghaduta

When he became a king, he used to go to Indraloka and worship Brahma. They were engaged in Prajapalan. Dyanna eaters used to wear divine clothes. If any sin was committed by them, the village of the village would be destroyed. Brahmins used to recite the Vedas. Parastri, Paradravya had turned away. The curse was the power of grace. Milk was taken 3 times from cows. The earth was perfect in all respects. Once sown, the crop was harvested seven times.

CHAPTER : - 6
PERIOD OF SHRI KRISHNA

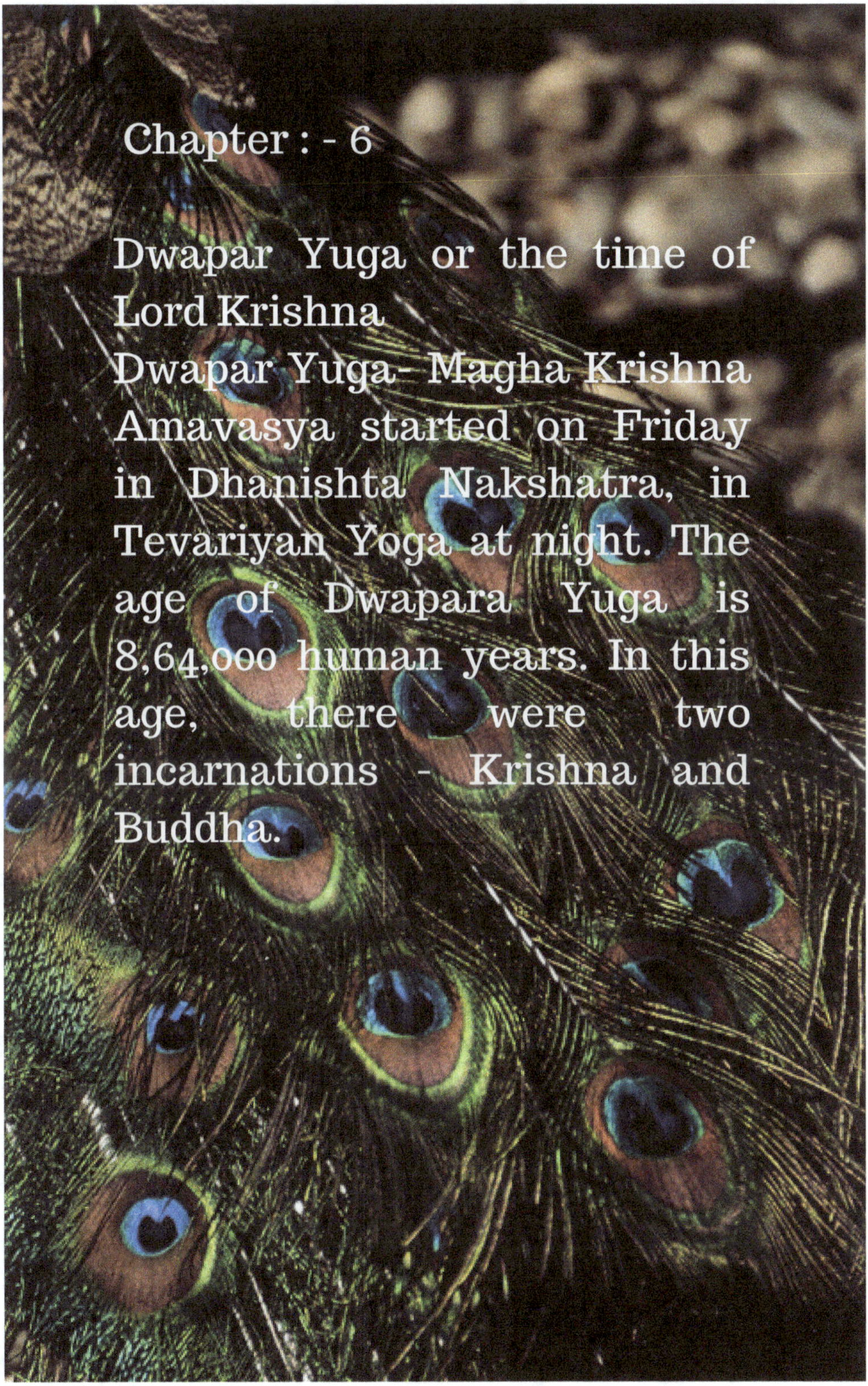

Chapter : - 6

Dwapar Yuga or the time of Lord Krishna
Dwapar Yuga- Magha Krishna Amavasya started on Friday in Dhanishta Nakshatra, in Tevariyan Yoga at night. The age of Dwapara Yuga is 8,64,000 human years. In this age, there were two incarnations - Krishna and Buddha.

1. Krishna Avatar- Bhadra Krishna Ashtami day occurred on Wednesday, Rohini Nakshatra, Nishith Kaal (midnight). This incarnation took place to kill the evil tyrant kings like Kansa and to protect the Gopa brothers.

2. Buddha - Ashwin Shukla was born on Thursday as the 10th incarnation. This avatar was taken to captivate the demons and bring peace to the people. Dwapar Yuga System - In Dwapar 10 sins, 10 gunas (samsara) human beings were 1000 years old, height was 7 cubits. Copper pot, rope material, and Kurukshetra was major pilgrimage place.

The skin was the last life women were respected. Solar eclipse 320, lunar eclipse 50. All the characters were engaged in their respective religious activities.

Dharma was established on earth in Dwapara Yuga in only two phases. In this age, Chandravanshi kings- Soma, Buddha, Pururava, Nal, Anus, Nahash, Shantanu, strange semen, Chitravirya, Pandu Yudhishthira, Abhimanyu, Parikshit, Bornjay.

His journey was up to Mount Sumeru. Divine food used to wear divine clothes. God was always ready to receive worship. Milk could be taken twice from cows. After sowing the crop was harvested 5 times. In that period, once the crop was sown once, when it was ripe, even after cutting it, it would grow again. The soil had such fertility.

CHAPTER : - 7
PERIOD OF UNRIGHTEOUS

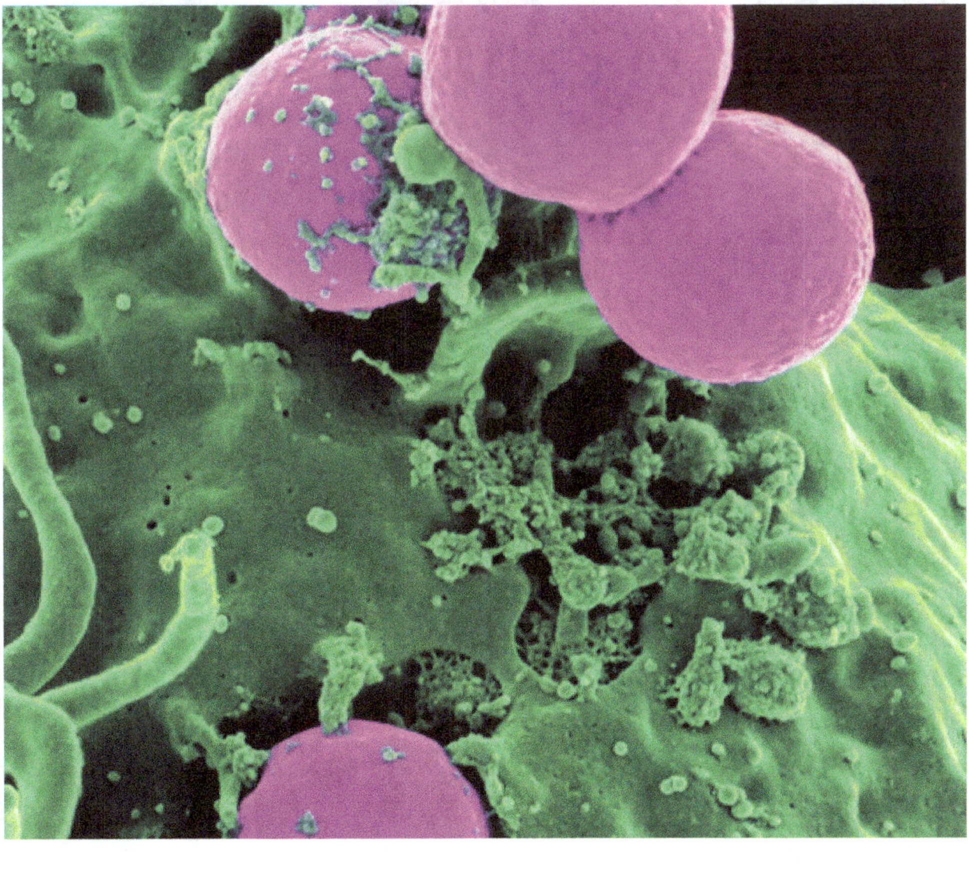

Time of the unrighteous Kaliyuga system.

The arrival of Kali Yuga took place at midnight on Sunday in Bhadra Krishna Trayodashi Sunday, Ashlesha Nakshatra and Vyatipata Yoga. The total age proof of Kali Yuga is 4,32,000 human years. In this, there will be an incarnation in the country of Sambhal (named Vishnu) by the name of Kalki in the house of Gaur Brahmin. Kaliyuga will have 15 sins, 5 virtues (world), human age 100 to 60 years, body height, 3 hands, clay and iron utensils, copper and iron material, Ganga pilgrimage and food life. The other parts of the Dharma will be completely neglected in Kali Yuga. People who tell lies will be liars. All the characters will be devoid of their respective karma.

The cow will give less milk. In Kaliyuga, the earth will be seedless, medicines will be tasteless. The lowly people will defame the sannyasa ashram by disguising themselves as sanyasi. There will be more solar eclipses and lunar eclipses. The king will give up his religion. Brahmins will be misled. Women will be anti-husbands, and sons will be anti-parents. There will be suffering everywhere in Kali Yuga. Dharma will remain in one place in Kali Yuga. The earth will become devoid of Ganga. People will worship ghosts, vampires etc. Bhagirathi Ganga has said – As long as I will continue to flow with you in the earth world. As long as Jupiter is situated in the constellation planetary system, I will not leave the earth.

I take a pledge to last for 10,000 years of Kali Yuga. At the beginning of Kali Yuga, the kings who run the six Shakas (Samvatsar) will be - Yudhishthira, Vikramaditya, Shalivahana, Vijayabhindan, Nagarjuna, Kalki king initially Yudhishthira Shaka, Chandravanshi king till 3044

Arjuna, Abhimanyu, Parikshit, Janamejaya, Vatsaraj, Yuvanshva etc. became kings. After this, the Suryavanshi kings were Ashwapati, Gajapati, Narpati, Mahipati, Mahipala, Mahendrapal, Gandharvasen etc. respectively. Happened after the New Year in the city of Ujjayini. Yudhishthira Saka became the king of Vikramaditya after 3044 years in the city of Ujjayini. He was 135 years old. Under this, Vikramaditya, Bhartrihari, Seni, Munj, Bhoja and Ramdev became kings. Shalivahana Shaka will last for 18 thousand years on the banks of Narmada, in which Shalivahana, Shalikumar, Kshatrak, Indrakrit, Brahmadivakar, Malimdatta, Gaudambak, Jayadeva, Shrimaddev, Narendra Shah will be 10 kings. After this, there will be the kingdom of the kings of the Yavan dynasty in which Timirling Shah, Babur, Humayun, Akbar, Jahangir, Aurangzeb, Bahadur Shah, Muhammad Shah, Ahmed Shah, Alamgir Shah, Shah Alam etc. will be the Yavan emperors. After the Yavanvanshi kings, Gauraganshi would rule over Queen Victoria, the seventh Edward, and the fifth George (English rule) the king of Tender.

There will be governments of looting, theft, dishonesty, rigging, treason, and defection. The bureaucracy will punch and oppress the poor people. Fake data, fake investigation, and fake justice will be rampant everywhere. The public will be dominated by incest atrocities. The saying "whose stick is his buffalo" will continue. Leaders will compete. Harijans will rule Kalki after the remaining 821 years, there will be an avatar of Kalki who will fix the deteriorating governance system. It Will work without policy. There will be governments of looting, theft, dishonesty, rigging, treason, and defection.

In this way, Hindu beliefs were told by their Bhavishya Purana thousands of years ago. And in fact, the events happened just like that. How great were the people of that time who used to know in advance all the happenings on the whole earth?

I do not know what the science they knew and today we do not know, in my view, the science of that time was even more advanced than today, but modern thinking made a big mistake considering it old and superstitious.

CHAPTER : - 8
POSSIBILITY OF
LIFE ON MARS

Chapter : - 8

Possibility of life on mars

"You told me such a long story and so deep", what does it mean?

 You are very smart - "Try to make your brain horse run faster"!

not much but I think yours somewhere else; not because of our search for life here. Absolutely! You got it right, Professor, my point was in this direction which you should be able to understand - 'John Kate'.

 On this basis I tried a lot to understand what is the matter;

That only one planet of our solar family has all the compatibility of life and why not in the rest? Some may have geographical reasons, such as distance from the Sun or others, but some of these are planets on which life could have been possible, but is not. There seems to be some historical reason behind this, which can also be related to these time cycles.

Professor Belen, You must have read the religious texts of Hindus, there are many stories in those texts where the people of the earth used to go to other planets in space. Such as Moon Lok, Heaven Lok, Surya Lok etc. Today we know those planets as Sun and Moon, but we do not know about a planet like heaven, where it was and then the secrets of those planets also lived. Whom people used to call deities such as - Suryadev, the god of the sun world, Chandradev, the god of the moon world, Yama, the king or god of Yama and Indra, the god of heaven. They used to come and go on the earth very easily in their special types of vehicles. This means that there was life on these planets when people used to live here. But I do not understand why it was not so now, what happened that life ended from those planets; And everyone is completely deserted now.

Thousands of crores of years ago some such event must have happened due to which everything has ended but no one is aware of it. No scientist would have done a complete study of those books properly, who is doing research like us, otherwise, this mystery would have been solved very soon. I have also read Mahabharata where I tried to pay a lot of attention to one thing but still failed. "What is that, John

Kate, "- Professor Belen asked. Have you seen your Shri Krishna serial on TV too? It must have been seen in it that when Lord Krishna was telling the things related to the soul to Arjuna in the eighteenth chapter, he had described the earth as the land of death, that is, the planet of death, the living beings of other planets have to take birth here only to die.

CHAPTER : - 9
ZERO LAW

Chapter : - 9

Zero law

The living beings of each planet have to complete the cycle of birth and death according to the law of creation and finally get free from this bondage which is called liberation. Shri Krishna has told a lot to Arjuna in the Bhagavad Gita, but I tried to understand only a few things.

I think people used to live on many planets at some point in time, but due to the cycle of time, they all became desolate and lifeless. Once on earth when I went to visit India. Then a priest of a temple told me about the time cycle that when the Kali cycle had started, it was sure to affect this entire solar family. It affected these planets before the earth and destroyed the lives of all of them and made them deserted. Now it's the last step on earth which seems to be true. According to that Pandit, it is now ruling the earth, as a result of which it will eventually destroy this earth as well. And as you are already aware that it has used carbon as one of its main weapons which are proving to be very lethal. It generates such an idea in the minds of the people that it is only entertainment to tell all these things to the people. People always ignore it, as a result of which people of the whole earth are facing climate change today.

Science always keeps on making discoveries and leaves the old, but until it can not find new, it remains stuck on the old discovery, Higgs is proof of that. Earlier the smallest particle was considered to be an atom or energy electron but now it is believed to be Higgs. Some people are also looking at it by connecting it with religion, but the scientific discoverer whose name was Higgs.

He was an atheist and he did not accept the idea of linking it with religion. What is the reason for this in detail, only his research can prove it? Nevertheless, it was circulated in many media that this discovery is the God particle, which means religious itself, God means particle of God.

CHAPTER :-10
SCIENCE AND
RELIGION

Chapter : - 10

Science and religion
According to Shiva Mahapuran, when the earth accepted Mahadev's tears, a big demon was born whose name was Andhakasur and he had a brother named Rohtang. When Andhakasur was killed by Shiva, Andhakasur's brother Rohitang came to avenge him, he wanted to destroy Shiva through sound i.e. music and wanted to avenge the death of his elder brother from Mahadev but Mahadev defeated him too. And later placed him on Mars. Now we can read to find that monster also on this planet but how I do not know this Professor. There is also a description of such an incident in the story, but it is probably a story from thousands of years ago.

Sometimes I also get confused in this argument. What is the matter? And when I studied some religious books, I came to know that this argument is also true in my opinion.

"How was that, - Kate," asked Professor Belen.

Professor As you know how our body is structured; The main in this is our brain and its spinal cord, in which there is a place which is of peace and joy and from here the intelligence along with the ether enters. This wisdom gives strength to the whole body and is also a factor in the creation of a new organism. It is not an element of this earth nor is it produced on any other planet. This is the same energy power which flows continuously on this whole creation and its source is considered to be only and only Lord Vishnu or whom we call Paramatma or Purush.

Because in this whole creation there is only one who is male, not the rest like the soul which is present in all living beings and without him the body is just a corpse. The word soul itself is "Drilling", so whatever body is in the soul, it is made of woman i.e. nature, even if a male form is found in that body shape, then it is also created from the elements of nature and nature itself is a woman. So according to Hindu beliefs, this entire creation is nature itself and the living beings in it are its children and it is negative.

It attracts the energy which is positive and it is present at one place in this universe whose energy is positive. It is stretched and spread over this whole world and keeps on entering the negative object or body that falls in its path. For this reason, the whole universe is kept in equilibrium, otherwise, this universe would have been scattered. In different religions, we call that God by different names but He is only because of Him this world is organized. But people do not understand this. They believe that my God is the greatest, my religion is the best and keeps quarrelling amongst themselves while he is one.

It attracts the energy which is positive and it is present at one place in this universe whose energy is positive. It is stretched and spread over this whole world and keeps on entering the negative object or body that falls in its path. For this reason, the whole universe is kept in equilibrium, otherwise, this universe would have been scattered. In different religions, we call that God by different names but He is only because of Him this world is organized. But people do not understand this. They believe that my God is the greatest, my religion is the best and keeps quarrelling amongst themselves while he is one.

At the same time, a signal came on his radio in the area he had tested. The atmosphere there is changing and the influence of radioactive substances is increasing. This change can ruin their years of hard work. Hey, what a message this is coming! John, just look, that's why I stopped you midway because since yesterday I was suspecting that some signals were coming in my device. What will happen now, will our dream remain incomplete?

CHAPTER : - 11
THE BOY OF ANOTHER SOLAR SYSTEM

Chapter : - 11

The boy of another solar system

Suddenly some voice started to be heard in his ears from the sky. It was of a vehicle, at once, both of them felt that perhaps a vehicle from Earth had been sent to them on Mars, but they did not know about it. How could this happen? A bewildered doubt began to appear on both of their faces. Both of them started looking up in the sky and after just a few moments a circular spacecraft lane near them on Mars

From there a boy got down. He looked very young, about twenty or twenty years old, he was not even wearing any such outfit which is necessary for astronauts. In appearance, he was very strong and fair in complexion, he looked exactly like the people of the earth. The surprising thing was that he was going very comfortably in the atmosphere there, walking freely like the atmosphere of the earth. I don't know how he was able to breathe there! Seeing him, John Kate and Professor Belen were very surprised, oh what! Who is there; this boy! Now the boy reached them to answer those questions.

Professor Bellen and John Cate were inside their tunnel and the boy got out of his vehicle and approached them. "He sent them and asked Iron with his own hands" - Who are you, where have you come from and what is all this? He spoke something but his language was different which those people could not understand but both of them understood the boy's gesture. The same question was also arising in his mind: who are you brother and who are like this; Arrived here, and even in this very comfortable environment, Professor Belen, speaking something in English, tried to explain it with his hands.

The sound was also reaching outside the tunnel which the boy could hear. He was familiar with English and now he understood that these people speak the English language. Now he asked in English only, who are you and what are you doing here? "The professor said, who are you brother and what have you come here to do?"

'The boy said, I Equesh was going somewhere while roaming in space, so I got your radio signal, following which I came here.' There is a similar solar system far away. This is exactly like this solar system, with nine similar planets revolving around a sun on which there is life on some planets.

CHAPTER : - 12
INHABITANTS
OF MARS

Chapter : - 12

Inhabitants of mars

I have come to know many such things about the earth, which you probably do not even know! But I did not believe that I would be able to see and meet you like this. By the way, I always used to search for your planet in this space but I could not reach it. There is a reason behind that which I will tell you later.

I am very happy now that I can help you in your search. I will also go to your planet from where you have come and try to improve that too. Squash's words brought a wave of happiness to the tunnel. He asked him a lot of information related to his search for life on Mars and said I will make his dream come true in just a few days, just keep watching.

Science has made a lot of progress from where I am. The work of the people there is now being done more in search of life on these new planets. We have settled our people on many other small and big planets. There was a reason behind not reaching here. A curse! I think it's over now; Otherwise, I would not have been able to reach here, as before, I would have wandered here again after coming here. By transmitting to my mind the machines of my vehicle are also conveying the secret that the danger is now over. Your dream will come true now.

"Equesh said"- You might not know about us but the people of our planet have complete information about your planet Earth. Because of that curse, our people considered it good to stay away from you, otherwise, our planet may also have to face danger. Otherwise, long ago our people would have met you and solved your problems very easily.

Now let's see what I do. Saying this he said you open the door to let me out of the tunnel. The door was opened, he came out of the tunnel and went to his vehicle, then after some time he got down from the vehicle and took something with him, it was a small box-shaped machine. Which he now placed on the surface of Mars and then turned on some of its buttons. After leaving that machine on the surface, he asked the professor to open the tunnel door and went inside to him. After going inside, Eqush told Professor Belen that tonight I will be here with you guys, and then in the morning, I will be able to tell you something about what test I have started. Then Eqush was introduced to the rest of the people in those tunnels during the night, a lot of talks happened and a good bed was arranged for him to rest. Now everyone is asleep as the night is longer.

When it was morning the next day, the scene there had changed. The dusty atmosphere had completely calmed down, the extreme heat was now over. The spread of harmful gasses had completely stopped and many more which were harmful to the human body were eliminated. The atmosphere there had now become such that there was no need for people to live inside the tunnels. ESquashwas still asleep while some people were getting up and assessing the sight. They were also discussing among themselves that Eqush must have done something through that machine, due to which the view is happening like this.

Professor Belen had also got up and was very happy to see all this sight. He was waiting for Equesh to wake up from his sleep because only he could lift the veil from all the mysteries. Their computers and machines were giving them indications that the outside environment was completely fine, yet everyone was waiting for Equche to wake up.

Now after some time, Eqush had also woken up from sleep. He now remembered that he had put out a machine that would change the atmosphere of Mars. He also now wanted to see the result of that test. When he came out of the tunnel, he found that his test was successful. He was very pleased and asked Professor Belen to come out of the tunnel. Professor Belen was afraid that if I went out of the tunnel, nothing would happen to him. Equus told Professor, now you and all your other people do not need to stay in these tunnels because I have fixed the environment here with this machine of mine. Don't be scared, please come out, you don't need to be afraid.

Once the professor felt scared, but he had become very confident about the equesh No matter what happens, I will go out of the tunnel and he will also get out. After coming out, he was surprised, now he felt the atmosphere there was exactly like the earth. No problem in breathing, no heat or effect of any harmful element or gas. The atmosphere there had completely changed. Professor Belen laughed out loud and thanked Equesh repeatedly for having done a miracle for him. He now asked everyone else inside the tunnel to get out. On receiving his orders, all the people inside the tunnels came out and started enjoying the atmosphere.

Everyone jumped with joy because their hard work was made possible very easily by equesh, and their dream came true. Professor asked Equesh how did you do this or that too in just one night? I am very surprised! How is this possible please tell me squash.

"Equesh" - Professor this is not a miracle but science was deserted. The scientists of our planet took a very long time to make this device. Till now many people have it, and I am one of them. This yantra has the power to fix the atmosphere of this planet only for a few parts, you will have to do the rest of the work by yourself, after which gradually the whole planet will be cured.

Now clouds will form here and there will be the rain of water; Your job will be to spread the seeds of different types of plants from place to place. Life can begin only from seeds. Only plants will be able to adapt to the entire environment here. Then all the people started waiting for the rain. After a few days, clouds started forming in the sky and there it rained like the earth. The professor, after asking his people, spread the seeds of plants there in the area indicated by Equate.

After this much happened, Equesh said that I have to go to my planet now. I will come here again later, till then there will be greenery all around here. Till then you will have to wait and he took farewell to all the people and flew into the sky in his spaceship. What was now, gradually time passed and people planted greenery of vegetation all around there.

Somewhere he had grown very big trees too. That too in a very short time which was very surprising but when we go deep into it it is no wonder, Eqush had given him the seeds of some trees which grow very fast, the secret behind this is their planet's People's knowledge of biodiversity technology. He had achieved the highest aptitude and success in this technique.

By changing the chromosomes of plants and trees, making their size micro and large. Techniques for growing plants and trees in less time and complex conditions. All this was the result of his advanced research on Biodiversity. Now the people here declared themselves the inhabitants of Mars and laid the foundation of civilization there. Sent a message to the earth and requested to fix its environment. Arrangements were made to bring the people of the countries whose atmosphere had become very hot.

BIO DIVERSITY WILL
CONTROL CLIMATE
CHANGE AND BRING
LIFE ON MARS

BIO DIVERSITY
ON MARS

HOW CAN BE POSSIBLE GROW PLANTS ON PLANET MARS GIVE WINGS YOUR IDEA

Fickt liebe
EINANDER ans
unseres PLANETE

BUDUCNOST
BL
"Be a PART OF
THE
SOLUTION
NOT PART OF
THE
POLLUTION"

SOLUTION OF POLLUTION CAN CONTROL CLIMATE CHANGE

SAVE MOTHER EARTH

STEP TO
MARS TO
SEARCH
LIFE FOR
NEW ERA
All photos are from
pixels and pixaways